This book is
dedicated to
Bill Yates, who
always encouraged me.

Published by Modern Publishing
A Division of Unisystems, Inc.

Copyright © 1978, 1980, 1987, 1988
Guy Gilchrist Productions, Inc.

MUDPIE AND HIS FAMILY™ and character names are
trademarks of Guy Gilchrist Productions, Inc.

® Honey Bear Books is a trademark owned by
Honey Bear Productions, Inc., and is registered in the
U.S. Patent and Trademark Office.

Printed in Spain

My Name Is Mudpie

by Guy Gilchrist

MODERN PUBLISHING
A Division of Unisystems, Inc.
New York, N.Y. 10022

My name is Mudpie and I'm 4½ years old. I live
in a yellow house with my Mom and Dad, my baby
sister Punkin and my best friend Trapper.

My other friends, Banjoey and Pawdette live right next door. We don't even have to cross the street to play together.

Banjoey, Trapper and I have a lot of
adventures together.

Sometimes we make fishing poles and go
fishing at the little creek behind our houses.

I just know that one day Banjoey, Trapper and I are
going to catch a whale!

We've already decided what we are going to do with him. We'll keep him in the bathtub and feed him french fries.

I'll also take him with me to kindergarten for "show and tell."

I could even put a saddle on him and ride him around the world! That's what I'm going to do when we catch our whale in the little creek.

But on days when I'm not playing outside, I like
to play in my room. My room is my favorite place in
the whole house.

The reason why I like my room best is because that's where I keep my toys, my books and all my secret stuff.

I also have my own bed where I go to sleep each night with my favorite blanket.

Sometimes I let my baby sister come into my room
to play with me. I pretend I'm the starship captain
and she's the first mate!

Another one of my favorite rooms is our kitchen.
My mom lets me use the table in there to work on
special projects for school. Punkin tries to help.

But most of the time, our family just eats there.

At night, I have to go into the bathroom and do things I don't like to do very much at all. I have to take baths and wash behind my ears, brush my teeth and clean underneath my fingernails too!

Then I get into my jammies and Mom makes sure I
kiss Punkin good night.

Afterwards, Dad reads me a story, tucks me in, kisses me goodnight and says, "Sweet dreams, Mudpie!"

Sweet dreams? Maybe! Or maybe exciting dreams or funny dreams! Who knows what I'll dream tonight! I better get to sleep so I can find out. Good night Trapper.

And good night to you too.